Towards the Light

Anamika Gopan

Ukiyoto Publishing
All global publishing rights are held by

Ukiyoto Publishing

Published in 2023

Content Copyright © Anamika Gopan
ISBN 9789360164690

*All rights reserved.
No part of this publication may be reproduced, transmitted, or stored in a retrieval system, in any form by any means, electronic, mechanical, photocopying, recording or otherwise, without the prior permission of the publisher.*

The moral rights of the author have been asserted.

This is a work of fiction. Names, characters, businesses, places, events, locales, and incidents are either the products of the author's imagination or used in a fictitious manner. Any resemblance to actual persons, living or dead, or actual events is purely coincidental.

This book is sold subject to the condition that it shall not by way of trade or otherwise, be lent, resold, hired out or otherwise circulated, without the publisher's prior consent, in any form of binding or cover other than that in which it is published.

This title is produced in Association with Pachyderm Tales

www.pachydermtales.com

ACKNOWLEDGEMENT

I whole heartedly thank,

Mohanasundari Jaganathan,

(Managing Director of Sharp Electrodes Pvt Ltd)

for funding this project.

Without her, this book would not be possible!

This book was a part of workshop conducted in our college, NGM College Pollachi and Pachyderm Tales.

I whole heartedly thank our management, our teachers and HOD of English Dept, NGM as well as Suja Mam for this initiative.

In a beautiful village called Muddenahalli, lived the Sharma family. It consisted of a mom, dad and two siblings.

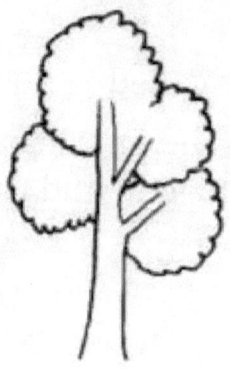

Appu was the eldest and naughtiest one. Adi was the little brother who was the quiet and innocent one. Appu was in 10th standard and Adi was in 5th standard.

Appu would make him carry all his books to their school. He would make him do his homework. Adi did everything for his brother with pleasure.

On a sunny Monday morning, both the brothers started to their school with Adi carrying the books as usual.

By the middle of the day, Appu got too bored by the classes and decided to bunk. But he could not get a proper reason.

After thinking for a while, he rushed to his brother's class. He called Adi and ran to the staffroom.

He informed the staff in charge that his brother was sick and asked

permission to take him to the doctor.

Poor Adi did not understand

anything.

Yet, he just shook his head at everything his brother said.

They got permission to take a day off. Appu was very happy. He took Adi and boarded the bus that took them to the town.

They went to the theater and watched a movie.

Appu bought them lunch from a nearby stall and had it. Later, they went to an art exhibition. It was held in the middle of the town.

They were wandering around the town, spending money lavishly. Adi told his brother that it was not good. He wanted to go back home.

But Appu did not listen to him. He ignored his little brother.

And when the sun was about to set, they boarded the bus back home. As it was a busy day, the bus was fully packed.

Appu had never been on such a crowded bus and the inexperience made him miss the stop.

They both got down in a strange place.

The bus slowly faded out of his sight before he could sense what was happening.

He didn't know where he was. And it was totally dark everywhere.

There weren't any streetlights either.

Frightened, Adi grabbed his
brother's hand.
But this time, Appu did not push him away. He too, was scared.

He finally started to regret his decisions. They spent a lot of time in the darkness.

There was a deep silence around the place. Suddenly, Appu saw a huge figure of shadow nearing them.

Appu grabbed his brother's hand and started running. They ran from the place, to save their lives from the shadow.

They were running as fast as they could. But he was too late. He heard a sharp cry and realized it was Adi's.

He turned around and was shocked to see a shadow grabbing Adi. He didn't know what to do. With sweat dripping and trembling legs, he tried to get Adi back from the shadow.

He shouted for help. But the shadow was stronger. It pushed him away and he fell with a thud. The pain was so severe that he fainted.

Even then, he was able to hear the faint voices of his brother. He was very happy to hear his brother again.

He wanted to see him and he tried to open his eyes. When he finally opened his eyes, he realized that all of this was just a nightmare.

His brother was all safe and was standing right in front of him,

getting ready for school.

Appu cried out of happiness. He hugged Adi tightly and apologized for all his ill treatment. He promised that he'd be a good brother from now on.

He also decided to be a good boy so that Adi would have a better role model. He attended his classes properly and topped the exams.

Adi started to follow his brother and he too turned into a perfect young man!

The Author

Anamika is currently pursuing a degree in English literature at the undergraduate level. When her mother, a teacher, read devotions and stories about kings, she grew up listening to them. In childhood, she read more books and would narrate them to her schoolmates at prayer. She would imagine things in her mind and draw them on paper. It was JK Rowling's Harry Potter that inspired her to write this story. She is an amazing artist too. Anamika herself is the illustrator of her first book. A fantasy and thriller writer, she enjoys writing stories in these genres.

www.ingramcontent.com/pod-product-compliance
Lightning Source LLC
LaVergne TN
LVHW041644070526
838199LV00053B/3547